THI

OF RAMÓN

& Other Stories from the Cantina

ALSO BY
GERVASIO ARRANCADO

SHORT STORIES

Eufemia and José

Maldito

Maldito & the Tourists

The Storyteller

The Man of Mud

Maldito & Tomás

COLLECTIONS

Stories from the Cantina

ALSO SEE WORKS BY

Gervasio Arrancado, Nicolas Z Porter,
Harvey Stanbrough, and Eric Stringer
Harvey Stanbrough & Friends Writing in Public
– http://HEStanbrough.com –

THE CYCLE OF RAMÓN
& Other Stories from the Cantina

GERVASIO ARRANCADO

FrostProof808 Publishing
Post Office Box 604
Saint David, Arizona, USA 85630-0604

First Edition, June 2014
Printed in the United States of America

ISBN-13: 978-1499762891(Paperback)
ISBN-10: 1499762895(Paperback)

Also available as an electronic book in all major ebook
outlets and formats.

ISBN: 978-1-311-95003-1 (Ebook)

Credits
Cover photo courtesy Shutterstock (Shutterstock.com)
Editing, formatting and cover design by Harvey Stanbrough
(HarveyStanbrough.com)

Disclaimer
This is a work of fiction, a product of the author's imagination. Any resemblance or similarity to any actual events
or persons, living or dead, is purely coincidental. Although
the author and publisher have made every effort to ensure
there are no errors, inaccuracies, omissions, or inconsis-
tencies herein, any slights or people, places, or organi-
zations are unintentional.

for those who long to visit
that place on the horizon
where reality folds into imagination
and for those who live there

CONTENTS

The Cycle of Ramón...................................... 1

Carmen, Whose Face Was Cracked........... 31

The Rabbit & the Priest: A Tale.................. 61

The Dawn of Rigoberto............................... 77

The Storyteller.. 89

About the Author.. 113

THE CYCLE OF RAMÓN
& Other Stories from the Cantina

GERVASIO ARRANCADO

THE CYCLE OF RAMÓN

The world had been sad for three days. The sky wept steadily, softly, the water drip, drip, dripping from limbs and leaves of trees and eaves of houses, trickling into rivulets and streams that whispered their way east, to the ocean. There was only the overcast and mist and rain, but no thunder. Only the gentle pattering of drops that seemed almost to hush each other as they washed houses and fences and gardens and roads and paths. Only the cool, mute darkness. The normally flashy lightning dared not rend the sky with so much as a single appearance, and in those few rare moments when a break appeared in the clouds, the stars dimmed themselves rather than risk interrupting the young widow's mourning.

Maria Elena leaned over the dining room table, which took up one whole end of the roomy kitchen, and gently stroked her husband's black, wavy hair. "*Ramón... mi Ramón,*" she whispered, her voice barely disturbing the air. "*Tu eres mi corazón.* You are my heart." As she had the past two nights, she dipped a soft linen cloth in a pan of hot water, squeezed it with one hand, then washed gently over his forehead. A matched pair of tears slipped from her cheeks and fell next to his nose. She creased the cloth to bring a fresh fold to bear, then smoothed his eyebrows from the center out, but was careful not to allow the linen to touch the tears, which had settled into the corners of his eyes and were no doubt seeping between his eyelids. "*Te amo, Ramón... mi corazón.*"

She carefully creased the cloth again and washed each temple, brushing his hair over his ear on either side. As another tear slipped from her cheek to his, she dipped the cloth in the water again, squeezed it, then gently washed his cheeks, creased the cloth and washed both jaws, his neck and throat and chin. Finally she dropped the linen cloth into the bowl and sighed. "*Le perderé para siempre, mi amor.* I will miss you for a very long time." She stood, picked up the bowl of tepid water and looked upon her husband, who seemed to have faded a great deal since yesterday, then shook her head and moved toward the kitchen. *How I wish he could simply awaken!* Among the many legends in her village, she had heard rumors of the dead awakening when the heavens openly wept for them, especially when lightning shows respect by its absence and even the stars avert their faces. She had heard of them living again when the tears of a loved one settled into the spirit path of their eyes. *No... Ramón is gone.* She dabbed lightly at her own eyes. *At least I've had a chance to say goodbye.*

A knock sounded lightly on the door, and Maria Elena set the bowl, cloth and all, on the kitchen counter alongside the sink and went to answer it.

Her mother, Federica, and her mother's sister, Juana, peered at her from beneath Federica's umbrella, their faces on an eerie cusp between the shadows of the night and the flickering glow emanating from the fireplace. Pushing Juana ahead of her, Federica closed her umbrella, then entered and enveloped her daughter in a warm but restrictive hug. Rainwater from the umbrella dripped on the saltillo tiles, discoloring the mortar between them. "We have been so worried about you, Maria! Are you all right?"

"I'm fine, Mama." Maria Elena shrugged away from her mother's arms and hugged Juana lightly to get it over with.

Juana's brow furrowed. "Are you sure you are okay, *Mija*? Not a word in three days!"

Her mother sighed and shook her head. "Nothing is going so well these days, eh?"

"Nothing has gone well for a very long time, Mama. But it's—"

Her mother brushed past her, followed closely by Juana. Federica removed her coat as she bustled into the kitchen. "Oh, how I've missed this kitchen!" She flopped her coat over the back of a chair and laid her umbrella on the table right between Ramón's legs. "Is there coffee?"

Maria blanched, retrieved the umbrella and hung it on a peg on the wall. "Of course there is coffee, Mama." She took a mug from the cabinet over the sink and turned to the stove. Just as she turned back with the coffee, Juana flopped her coat across the table, effectively covering Ramón's lower abdomen. Maria Elena screeched as the hot coffee sloshed from the cup and scalded a rivulet across the back of her hand. An instant later the cup shattered on the floor, and in the next instant she'd covered the distance to the table. "I'm so sorry, Mama. I'll get you another cup in a moment." She grabbed Juana's coat and flung it over the back of a chair, then returned to the stove, her legs gone weak and her voice having assumed a trembling quality. "Perhaps... we should take our coffee in the living room?" She poured a cup and turned to the women, then handed the mug to her mother. Regaining her composure a bit, she said, "*Y Tia Juana,* would you care for a cup?"

The two women looked at her oddly for a long moment, as if an evil twin was peering at them from behind her ear, and the only sound was the cruel, popping, staccato laughter from the fireplace in the next room. Her mother set her cup on the table, nearer Ramón's left ankle than his right, then reached to caress her daughter's arm. "We just worry, *Mija.* It's that time of year again." Just as quickly she pulled her hands back to herself and bit her lip. Then, in a very quiet voice, she said, "He's gone, *Mija*. You know he's gone, yes?"

Tears brimming in her eyes, Maria Elena nodded. "*Si*, Mama... and everything will be all right. What cannot be remedied—"

Her mother caressed her arm. "Yes, yes. That is the truth of things."

Her Aunt Juana caressed the other. "Remem-ber, *todo es posible con Dios, Maria*. With God, all things are possible."

"Yes, yes... everything will be all right." She retrieved her mother's coat from the back of the chair, and the umbrella and Juana's coat from the pegs. "For now, though... for tonight... I must complete my private mourning."

Her mother took her coat and sighed. "Yes... of course you must decide for yourself what is proper and right." She hugged Maria and looked closely at her daughter's face. "We will see you soon, then?"

Maria wiped a tear from her cheek, the only one she'd allowed to escape in her mother's presence in over five years. "I will see you soon." She saw them to the front door, closed it gently behind them, then turned the latch and returned to the dining room table. She pulled out a chair, sat, and lay her head on her husband's shoulder. "*Ramón... mi Ramón... mi corazón. Regrese por favor.* Please come back to me." But she knew that wouldn't happen. As sobs wracked her body, she thought back to the evening she'd known the love of her life.

*

Long before her parents had begun encouraging her to find a man of her own, to marry and have children, she and Ramón had run down to the sea almost every day after their lessons. The son of a stone mason, Ramón took his lessons at his home very near the center of the village and from his next door neighbor, a priest who was teaching him to write in two languages. Maria Elena took her lessons, primarily in sewing and cooking and the tending of a home, in her parents' house, which was situated just above the beach as necessitated by her father's station as a somewhat successful fisherman, sometimes.

Because of the location of their houses in

relation to the sea, most often Ramón would come get her, though it seldom seemed like that. A very physical boy, he would run from his house all the way to the beach, the better part of three kilometers, but as he came nearer to her little stone and mud house, he would slow his pace. It was their secret, their way of him picking her up without making a fuss of the whole thing and including parents and friends and other outsiders. He knew he belonged with her, and she knew she belonged with him, and what anyone else knew or did not know was of no consequence.

Over all those years, from the time he was six and she was five until he was fifteen and she was fourteen, most days found her waiting for him in the front yard, perched on the stone fence "like a little bird," her father said and then waved as he headed off to the cantina to relax from his arduous day and her mother, inside, fingered her rosary, nimbly moving from one bead to the next, and mumbled quietly in the dark corner near the fireplace. From the time Ramón came over the hill from town and veered east-northeast past her house, he seemed almost suspended in time. Seeing such a beautiful physical specimen slowed to such a degree, his bronzed arms and legs pumping in slow motion, muscles tensed but seeming almost to hang in midair, always invoked a kind of sadness in her, as if it were a great, raw omen.

Then a grin would spread across her face and she would launch herself from her perch and catch up with him, at which time they both whisked away, laughing, covering the final 200 meters at full speed. Secretly, she had ardently suspected they covered that remaining distance at very near light speed. They swam and laughed and explored and built sand castles and could not imagine that anything sinister would ever enter their lives.

*

Maria awoke, looked at her beautiful Ramón. He was growing more pale, as if fading. She caressed his hair. "Do you remember, Ramón, when Francisco called me *Cara Pequeña de Puerco*? Little Pig Face?" She smiled. "You defended my honor well, my love. It was the first time you declared by your actions that I belonged to you and no other. I think I will never forget the look on Francisco's face when he stepped back and apologized."

*

Francisco was an apprentice stone mason in training with Ramón's father. As Ramón was sweeping up the leavings of the day, Francisco grinned mischievously. "You spend much time with Maria Elena de Cordoba. Perhaps someday you will marry her and no longer have to perform woman's work."

Bent to the task at hand, Ramón didn't realize the comment was intended as an insult. He shrugged. "I spend much time with many people. Maria is my friend. I work for my father. I do the tasks assigned to all apprentices... the same tasks you performed until a year or so ago. There is no woman's work or man's work. There is only work." He looked up.

Francisco sneered. "Still, it would be better to have *Cara Pequeña de Puerco* doing the sweeping and the sewing and cooking... and perhaps other things, eh?"

Ramón dropped the broom and balled up his fists. "What did you say?"

Ramón's father came in. "I heard what was said. You both come with me."

The boys followed him out the door and down the street to the village rectory, where he paused and knocked on the door.

The priest, Father Pablo, opened the door and listened as Ramón's father conveyed the earlier conversation. He looked at Francisco. "Do you wish to apologize for having insulted the honor of young Ramón's friend?"

Francisco vehemently shook his head.

The priest looked at Ramón and shrugged. "Surely you do not wish to fight him, so—"

Ramón's gaze never left Francisco's face. "Yes, Padre, I do wish to fight him."

Ramón's father tried to intercede. "But he is older than you, Ramón, and larger and stronger."

Ramón shook his head. Quietly he said, "He is not stronger, Papa. He is merely more brash. I will fight him."

Ten minutes later as Ramón, thirteen, and Francisco, fifteen, were getting set to do battle in the street outside the rectory, a small crowd had begun to gather. The village seldom saw such excitement in the late afternoon. Indeed, it was late enough and the rumors loud enough that Maria had left her perch and wandered into town to find her tardy friend. The crowd had attracted her, but once she recognized the boys in the circle, she faded back and remained mostly out of sight near the corner of the rectory.

Father Pablo made a show of announcing the reason for the dispute. The fact that young Ramón was willing to fight an older, much larger boy to defend the honor of his friend—his *girl* friend—was not lost on the females in the crowd. The padre was instructing the boys in the rules of the contest. "There will be no kicking or clawing, do you understand? No biting, and no gouging to the eyes. There will also be no—"

Francisco interrupted the priest with the first punch, a hard blow that caught Ramón on the left cheekbone, snapping his head to the right and glancing off his nose just enough to cause a trickle of blood.

Ramón grinned broadly, partly to show off for the girls among the small crowd circling around him and Francisco, but mostly with pleasure. He sensed the punch was Francisco's best shot, and it had only barely stung him.

The priest stepped back in awe, his mouth open. "Francisco! It was not time to begin! It was not time!"

Never taking his gaze from Francisco, Ramón raised one hand and the priest stopped. Ramón glared at Francisco, blood trickling over the slight smile on his lips, and motioned him forward with a cocked index finger.

Eyes set in slits, Francisco approached him, not realizing he was on the verge of defeat.

The priest advanced as well, ready to intervene if necessary.

Blood streaming from his nose, Ramón stuck his face close to Francisco's left ear. His smile tempered his words. "You cannot hurt me. You will step back. You will apologize aloud to Maria Elena... who is my woman... or we will finish this."

The priest stepped back quickly, barely able to contain his own smile.

A red spot soaked through Francisco's white linen shirt at the shoulder. A sea breeze swept up the hill from the ocean, but even as the sweat cooled Francisco's brow, the spot on his shoulder grew warmer, almost hot. Almost imperceptibly, he nodded, his gaze locked with Ramón's, then stepped back. He tested Ramón's eyes for a moment, found stone-solid resolve, and bowed his head for a long moment. When he looked up, he spoke quietly but loudly enough for everyone in the circle to hear. "My sincere apologies, Ramón, for having made such a crude comment concerning Señorita Maria Elena de Cordoba." A slightly sarcastic tone crept into his voice as his fists tightened at his sides. "I did not understand that she was... *su cariñosita*."

Ramón nodded almost imperceptibly.

Francisco bowed again, low, then righted himself. "I am in your service." He took another step backward, then spun on his heel and went off down the road. He did not show up for his apprenticeship the next morning, and nobody in the village ever saw him again.

*

Maria stroked Ramón's hair again, noting that she could barely feel it. "You were my strong, handsome defender, Ramón. You were and are the love of my life, and it shall ever be so."

*

On the sixteenth anniversary of Ramón's birth, at the end of the workday, his father greeted him with a broad smile. "Today, my son, you are a stone mason. I can teach you nothing more. You have learned to speak and write English as well, so you can choose the life you live and where you live it. I hope you will remain in the village or at least nearby, but the world is at your feet. Ramón, I am proud of you."

Ramón embraced his father. "Gracias, Papa!" He stepped back, but could hardly contain his grin. "You will excuse me, Sir? I should probably—"

His father shook his head and burst into laughter, gesturing toward the door. "Go, my son, and be swift! She is waiting, probably perched on the fence as usual."

Ramón raced along the path to the east just as he did most days. But this day was different. He grinned broadly. This day he would stop short of the sea. This day he would ask Señor Cordoba to allow him to court his daughter. Then, in a year, once he had proven to her parents that he was worthy of her, he would ask for Maria Elena's hand in marriage. Of course, her father would give his assent and her mother would be ecstatic to have a stone mason in the family. There would be a huge engagement party. They would be married a year after that in the grandest wedding the village had ever seen. He leapt for joy and doubled his pace.

As he came over the edge of the hill and cut east-northeast from the trail, he did not slow down as usual. If anything he sped up, wanting to reach her, to pick her up and swing her in the air, to tell her he was a stone mason, to talk with her father, her mother. Then, if there was time and if it was still proper, they would go down to the sea together.

*

For Maria Elena, an unearthly sound brought the beginning of realization: a sharp, flat crack, like the strongest, most surprising bolt of lightning. She started to leap from the fence, her eyes stretched wide, her mouth trapped in a scream that might never end, and she watched Ramón slow down as usual, but not for the usual reason. She and he simultaneously hung in mid-air, trapped together in an excruciatingly long moment of horror but separated by eternity, her feet straining to reach the ground so she could run to him, wrap him up, protect him, just as a reddish-pink cloud appeared next to his head. As her feet touched the ground he pitched forward into the earth, never to move again.

*

Her father died two years later of a liver affliction, and her mother moved to the other side of the village to live with her sister. Maria chose to remain in the stone house near the sea, where, over time, she developed a habit of going down to the sea.

There, after dark so nobody could see, she would walk along the shore with Ramón, his hand on her waist, her head on his shoulder, and they would swim.

Of course, she knew he wasn't really there, but she kept hoping he would be. She prayed one night he would show up, take her in his loving arms, and pull her into the sea where they would reside together forever. Such is the way of love that has lasted over many lifetimes.

*

Four nights ago as I write this account, five years to the day after Ramón was murdered, it happened.

The sea beckoned, much more strongly than usual. Maria Elena ran down to the shore, stopped and peered into the darkness. She was alone, but if others had come along she wouldn't have noticed. Tonight there was something different... something more. She trembled, not with fear but with nerves, something she had never done when anticipating an evening with the sea. She pulled her blouse over her head and dropped it on the sand, then stepped out of her flowing skirt and her underwear and sandals. She waded out from the shore, closed her eyes and dove beneath the waves, gracefully stroking, her hands smoothly slicing through the water as if caressing its heart.

Where she sensed the water was getting deeper, she stood again, peering out into the gentle waves, her arms slightly above her head, almost as if in surrender. *I would surrender to the sea*, she thought. It was such a wonderful place, a living entity. Ships had sunk there, and airplanes, and lovers had drowned there. It was alive with wild creatures as well, but also with beings from above.

Countless times she'd seen the small fireballs in the sky arcing perfectly toward the sea. Sometimes, she imagined, she heard Ramón laughing, no doubt with pure, heavenly ecstasy, for certainly he was an angel now. On those nights when she heard his laughter, she rushed to the shoreline and dove in quickly, immersing herself in the elation carried in the joyful waves. She could swim for hours on those nights, and when she left the water, she did so with a heart made lighter with joy, and she often smiled for the next few days.

At other times she heard heart-wrenching sobs and imagined a few immortals had chosen to drown their sorrows in the sea. On those nights, she knew Ramón was busy caring for his fellow angels. On those nights she did not swim. She did not want to interrupt her love in his important work, and she would not risk being overcome with celestial sadness. Her human mind and emotions, she was sure, would not be able to handle it.

Of course, her musings had a strong basis in fact. In her small village one legend held that an angel, a very old man with enormous wings, had fallen from the sky and ventured into a family garden to molt and rest and renew itself. Surely if an angel had fallen into her village, many more had fallen into countless other towns and cities and nations. And how many more must have fallen into the vastness of the sea? And they and the other creatures, in concert with the rhythms of the universe and the phases of Luna, had imbued the sea with true life: its own throbbing heartbeat, its own gentle rhythms. She felt most natural when surrounded by its swirling, watery tendrils, when receiving its loving caresses. Tonight would be special. She just knew it. Then the realization hit her: *Tonight Ramón is coming home to me!*

She waded deeper, her feet alternately touching sand, then giving way to weight-lessness. *This is how Ramón must feel all the time*, she thought. *Flowing, weightless, everywhere at one time.*

The waves rolled in gently, one after another after another, each soothingly warm, kissing her cheeks and chin, massaging her shoulders and throat, flicking around her small, buoyant breasts. Beneath the surface, the undercurrents paid homage, caressing her ankles and calves, swirling about her thighs and hips, stroking and circling her abdomen and waist.

Her eyes closed, Maria Elena sighed, never having felt such remarkably gentle yet electrifying sensations, and with something akin to reverence rested her arms on the surface. She reached to embrace her lover and whispered, *"Venga a mi, mi amor.* Come to me."

The currents swelled and warmed, swirling more strongly, firmer in their intensity, their heat embracing her, at once enveloping and penetrating her. She half-opened her eyes for only a moment, then closed them again and lay back, her lips curled in a soft smile as the sea's rhythm washed over her, kissing her forehead, her eyelids, her ears and throat and lips. It caressed her shoulders and arms, her back and abdomen, her hips and thighs and calves and feet. It bathed her, worshiped her, loved her.

Her passion matched that of the undulating, untamed sea, and it surged and swelled and heaved around her, into her, through her, caressing, twirling, swirling, writhing, undulating, whitecaps frothing, her breath quickening into gasps as her great lover finally, finally, finally began to ebb. Three hours after she'd ventured into the surf, she slept, one with Ramón and completely at peace as he carried her along to the shore. He lay her gently next to her clothing, then faded back into the sea.

She awoke a few hours later, her heart filled, her mind and body satisfied. She looked at the sky, the few wispy clouds, so thin that their passing only dimmed the stars, and only momentarily. She'd had an amazing dream, one in which every fiber of her being had been inundated, permeated, saturated with pure love, and she knew Ramón had been there. She'd been filled with light, every cell transformed into something better than it had been.

She finally sat up, pulled her knees to her chest, and clasped her hands in front of them. She looked at the beautiful sea, sparkling beneath the full light of Luna. *And he loves me so much, he caused me to sleep.* That had never happened before. She tried on a frown, but it wouldn't stay. She tried to feel sad that she'd slept so long, but there was no sense of loss or sadness at parting. Because *he is with me... he is still here.* She remembered how he used to wade just offshore, then plop down, immersing himself completely, yet still within reach. And it dawned on her: *That's what he's done this time! He's right here! Right here!* Somehow, she felt only unbridled joy, as if it emanated from her very core.

The sky beyond the edge of the sea began to grow light and she knew she must hurry. This might be the last chance she would have to say a proper goodbye to her love.

She put on her panties and sandals, then swept up her skirt and blouse and waded into the surf. A warmth caressed her legs. *Here.* She smiled. *He's right here.* She stooped and soaked Ramón into her skirt and blouse. When she was sure she had all of him, she waded out of the surf and walked up the path to her small stone house.

Just as the sun peeked over the horizon, she closed the door, kicked off her sandals, and carried Ramón to the dining room table. She released him from her blouse and skirt, then tossed those over the back of a chair and turned back to him. He looked so handsome lying there.

She leaned over the dining room table, which took up one whole end of the roomy kitchen, and gently stroked her husband's black, wavy hair. "*Ramón... mi Ramón,*" she whispered, her voice barely disturbing the air. *"Tu eres mi corazón."*

*

As intricately connected as they were, Ramón himself became aware of a certain reduction, a letting go followed by an ebbing of himself and the tides in his cells, a wafting away of the need for sensory stimuli, then the rapid distancing of the stimuli itself.

His hearing and eyesight didn't fade as he'd always thought they would. Instead, those things to which he tried to listen or upon which he tried to focus quickly withdrew, receding to mere pinpoints of sound and light as quickly as a snapped finger. Still, he seemed able to sense their digression from here to there through their quantum trick.

Simultaneous with this reduction, Ramón experienced a kind of draining, a funneling from something into nothing, perhaps to make Nothing more full, or perhaps more empty. Even as he drained, he became the flow that accompanies being drained. At that moment a numbing, half-hearted deadness— a throbbing, pulsing, liquid kind of gravity—

pinned him and his numbness to a dark, stark, undulating mass.

At almost the same time the despondent grief of she who was letting go washed through him in a series of waves, gentle as the caress of a loving hand. The undulations were almost physical. He welcomed them, absorbed them, taking them into himself and far away from her.

Each wave began at the center of his forehead, smoothing out and down, out and down, out and down, descending over his eyelids, over and around his nose and eyes, down over his cheeks. Each wave lingered for an extra beat at his lips as if encountering a breakwater and mournfully regretting the need to surmount it, then slipped as if with remorse down over his chin, throat and torso.

Each wave continued through each limb and out through the tips of his fingers and toes. Of all the waves, the first was by far the strongest, and although each followed the same pattern, each washed through him with less intensity than the one before, merging him more fluidly into the liquid gravity that had been above and the undulating mass that had been below.

Even as the waves washed one after another through his body, tendrils from the first wave rose through his brain, probing, touching off electrical impulses, a grand finale to his personal fireworks show. Synapses fired in sequence, dozens setting off hundreds setting off thousands. Through a misty fog he flashed from a dark red warmth through light to crib slats and saltillo tile floors to jeans with a rope belt and friends and laughter and a wayward cursing of a coward with a gun and a brilliant, screaming-red instant and—synapses fired, thousands setting off millions setting off billions. He must have glowed like a shooting star, he thought, as he plunged from the heavens into the undulating mass of the womb.

Then the waves ebbed, dwindling to ripples, and just as he and the gravity and the undulations fully blended, the ripples lessened, lessened, lessened and blinked out of existence. The mist dissipated, and the mass he had become rose and fell, swelled and ebbed.

Something in his blood began to mix with his need. He began to dissolve. Bit by seeping bit he slipped through the slats in the table, then reconstituted beneath. He—the first bit of him—ran along the slats and dripped to the floor even as the next bits above were dissolving, slipping through slats, dripping to the floor and into a rivulet, tracing a path to the drain in the back wall.

In a few hours he was just in front of the garden and stretched around the corner to the shed and from there back through the drain where the last of him was seeping across the floor. And from the old, tired garden gate that he'd meant to fix after the honeymoon, from there back around almost to the shed, the water from the weeping sky dripped from limbs and leaves of trees and eaves of houses and trickled into rivulets and mixed with Ramón into streams.

There it was and there they were, the rainwater and Ramón, a stream bound in nature of nature, and it whispered its way east, toward the ocean.

The overcast and mist continued for his protection, but the lightning, no longer able to contain its joy at the reunion of life with life, flashed across the sky in bright smiles as the thunder applauded his return to the sea and from there to the heavens and from there, someday, to another womb. The stars burst like supernovae, celebrating.

By daybreak even the young widow, Maria Elena de Cordoba, had stopped mourning, for there was nothing to mourn. She couldn't remember a time when she hadn't been alone, and she could not remember ever being happier.

* * *
*

CARMEN,
WHOSE FACE WAS CRACKED

Clad happily in colorful linen skirts, a white blouse and a light cape with a hood pulled forward over her face, Carmen swept through the streets of Aguafuertes smelling delightfully of cinnamon and burnt sugar from the pastries she had helped her mother make after breakfast. There also was a headier, deeper scent about her, an aura, but of aroma rather than wave lengths of light from the rare end of the spectrum. She smelled of beauty and of innocence.

She couldn't have known that the day the soldiers rode into her village would be her last day on earth as a girl, that the humid evening to follow would serve as the threshold to womanhood, that she truly would never be the same again. The slightest smile curled her lips. *If I had known, I would have done nothing differently except that I would have gone to him more quickly, given myself to him more fully!*

*

The day before that most fateful day, Carmen's father, Eleazar Dominguez, the alcalde, had received word in his office that the village was in the path of a small contingent of cavalry and that they probably would arrive late the following afternoon.

According to the spies, the soldiers had been away from their homes for almost three months; they were battle weary from dealing with Apaches on one hand and rebels on the other; they had not stopped even for a drink and a civilized meal for over a month; and Aguafuertes was their last chance to stock their saddlebags and enjoy a night of relaxation before the final two-week march back to their home base.

This would be good news in almost any small, out of the way village like Aguafuertes because of the money the soldiers would bring to the town's coffers, but it was good news of a very different type for the alcalde. The spies had said the soldiers were being led by a young *capitan primero* whom one of them was certain was Antonio Guerrero.

The alcalde's eyes grew wide. "Are you sure, Pablo?"

The spy, who was much older than the others and only a couple of years younger than the alcalde, nodded. "*Sí, mi alcalde.* It is the son of Coronel Rafael Guerrero. He looks exactly like his father, but more so."

*

Seeking adventure, as young teenagers Pedro and Eleazar were filled with romantic dreams of serving the revolution. When they went rabbit hunting a few times each week in the early morning hours with Eleazar's father's old bolt-action rifle, it was always the same. They would move quietly among the mesquite and creosote and sagebrush, pretending they were sneaking up on a soldier made unaware of their presence by his own thoughts of all the defenseless peasants he had killed. When they scared up a rabbit they would freeze just as if they'd spotted a soldier, and they would crouch low to study the enemy. The doomed rabbit would run a short distance, then stop and stick both ears straight up as if he were tired of living and anxious for Eleazar's mother's cookpot. For a moment the two boys would imagine a sound had caught the soldier's attention and he had become wary, moving rapidly into what he erroneously thought was a safe and defensible position.

Eleazar would take careful aim at the bottom of the V formed by the rabbit's ears, then squeeze the trigger carefully. The rabbit would kick high in the air and fall to the earth dead at about the same time the imaginary soldier would crumple to the ground. The fantasy, thus expanded to a satisfactory conclusion, would end and the boys would return home with their bounty, talking all the way about how much easier and more fulfilling it would be to put a bullet through a member of the Mexican army than a rabbit. After all, the rabbit would feed a family for the night, but a dead soldier would feed the revolution for years to come.

On the days when no rabbits were forthcoming, the boys often crept up a the back of a boulder-strewn hillside above a well-used trail where they lay in wait for a column of cavalry. Of course, the column never showed up, at least not before the novelty of the fantasy had worn off beneath the heat of the day and the boys had left the hillside.

But one day, as misfortune would have it, when the boys had lain in the shadow of a boulder for over two hours and just as they were about to leave, Eleazar heard something. He motioned to Pablo to be silent.

Pablo crouched and froze in place. "What is it?"

"Shh! Horses I think!" Eleazar glanced at him, a grin spreading across his face. "This is our day, Pablo! It's the cavalry!"

"Are you sure?"

Eleazar, who had slipped onto his belly and slithered forward to peer around the boulder, motioned for Pablo to join him. He pointed. "See? Just there. Riding in two columns, and some sort of banner in front. That's cavalry!"

Pablo lay silent for a moment, watching the column approach. "Perhaps this is not a good idea, Eleazar. There are so many of them!"

Eleazar didn't even look around. "No. It is fate. We have been up here many times and nobody has slipped into our ambush. These men were meant to be here. Today is our day to prove our loyalty to the revolution. Give me the rifle."

Pablo made sure there was a round in the chamber, then passed the rifle forward. He whispered, "It's ready. I wish we had another rifle."

"It will be all right. I'll shoot a few and they will scatter, like in the stories we hear from the men in town when they've had a little to drink. Once they scatter, we'll slip back down the hill and disappear into the washes." The troop was almost directly beneath them. Eleazar glanced over his shoulder. "Are you okay?"

Pablo shrugged. "Sí. Your plan sounds right to me."

Eleazar took careful aim and sent a bullet into young private's thigh—shooting a cavalryman on horseback was more difficult, as it turned out, than shooting a rabbit who was bent on suicide—but the soldiers did not scatter. In what seemed like an evaporated second, four members of the troop peeled away and formed a guard around their wounded colleague. At the same time, the leader of the troop called a halt, drew his sword, turned the remainder of the troop to face the hill, and charged his attackers.

The sound of the pounding hooves and the yelling men was deafening. Eleazar, in his haste to escape, stumbled over Pablo and dropped the rifle, which clattered to the rocks in front of him and discharged. The bullet ricocheted off another boulder and smashed Eleazar's left kneecap. As he collapsed, holding his knee and moaning, Pedro tripped over him and fell into the dust alongside his friend. "What are we going to do now, Eleazar?"

"Shh! I don't know! It will be all right."

The thundering hooves and yelling voice had gone quiet, and no shots had been fired except that first one from Eleazar's rifle and then the accidental discharge. The only sounds were the boys' labored breathing, which was made louder by their attempts to stem it, and the almost stealthy sound of horses and men moving carefully among the rocks. The dust had almost settled around the frantic, whispering boys when the coronel rounded the boulder on his mount, his sword still drawn.

His eyes widened with recognition. "Why, you're only children!" He sheathed his sword and dismounted, handing his reins to a soldier who had come up behind him, then turned back to Eleazar with a slight bow. "Coronel Rafael Guerrero... why did you fire on my men? This could have been a very bad day for you, young señores."

Pablo's mouth opened, but nothing came out.

Eleazar pulled himself up to stand on his good leg and faced the coronel. He had intended to proclaim that he and his friend were members of the revolution, that the dictator and all his soldiers should burn in hell, but something deep in the man's eyes— a recognition of Hell, perhaps, or maybe just a vast sadness and wisdom—made him hold his tongue. There was no joy in those eyes, no peace, and certainly no fear. Eleazar swallowed and averted his gaze. "*Lo... lo siento, señor. Lo siento mucho.* I am very sorry. My friend and I... we were hunting rabbits. A shot went wild." He looked at the ground, a new sensation beginning to take root in the pit of his stomach. A quick glance at the coronel told him the man knew he was lying.

"Are you sure, *hermanito*? Do you and your friend perhaps fancy yourselves part of the revolution? You were very brave, but you did not do much harm. Surely the court would show leniency to a pair of boys so young."

And that attempt by the coronel to restore Eleazar's pride was the greatest transgression the boy would ever know, for the reality of who he was rendered him unable to take advantage of it. Anger filled his eyes. "We were shooting for rabbits, señor, and that is the whole of it. Since you believe us part of the revolution, you may keep my rifle."

The coronel looked at him for a long moment and a sad hardness crept across his face. He knelt and picked up the old rifle, then worked the bolt, ejecting the spent shell and loading another cartridge. He handed the rifle to Eleazar. "You keep your rifle." The coronel searched Eleazar's gaze again, then sighed. "Certainly you are no danger to me or my men. In the future, be more careful with your aim." With that, Coronel Rafael Guerrero turned his back on the boys, retrieved his horse, mounted and slowly led his soldiers back down the hill and on to their destination.

The boy Eleazar Dominguez watched as they rode away, hatred smoldering in his eyes. "I should kill him."

Pablo just looked at him. "We should get you home. Your mother will want to tend that leg."

*

Alcalde Eleazar Dominguez extrapolated the obvious: the soldiers might well stop in Aguafuertes for an evening of relaxation. After all, his was a small, friendly village of hard-working men, beautiful women, and chubby children. The village contained none of the bullet-scarred adobe buildings that so often marked rebel villages, and no soldiers had visited here officially. A plan began to form in his mind, and he worked on it late into the night. As he lay down on the sofa in his back office to get a few hours rest, he grinned. *They will expect nothing.*

*

The following morning, the alcalde picked up his cane and leaned heavily on it as he limped out of his office. Outside, he motioned to several boys. When they gathered around him, he said, "Run. Go to the fishing boats at the dock, to every farm, and to every business and home in the village. Tell the men to meet me in the cantina in one hour."

When the men had all arrived and the murmuring had died down, the alcalde stood and tapped his cane hard on the floor to get their attention. "My friends, the time has come for Aguafuertes to shine as a jewel in the revolution! Songs will tell of this day, when the men of our brave village set upon and destroyed those who would force upon us the tyrannical will of our oppressors!"

The men cheered halfheartedly, wondering who among them had been oppressed. Still, the alcalde was an excellent speaker. One man raised his hand. "Alcalde, is it a large force? How will we overcome them?"

"From all reports it is just the right size: small enough that with the element of

41

surprise and superior tactics we will destroy them, and large and well-trained enough that our descendants will sing of our victory for generations to come." He tapped his temple with his right index finger. "We will outsmart them, and we have Right on our side! We will overcome them with our cunning!"

Another man raised his hand. "Are they not excellent marksmen?"

"Perhaps, but marksmanship does not matter in close quarters."

And another, from the back. "Are they not also battle hardened?"

"Ahh, but also battle weary." He held up one hand to allay further discussion. "My friends, we must make our stand here." He tapped the floor hard with the tip of his cane. "Right here in the cantina. They will ride into our village this very afternoon. They will water their horses at our troughs and feed them with our oats, and then they will come here, to our cantina, where they will satisfy their physical thirst with our tequila and their immoral, animal lusts with our women! They will room in our small hotel and even in our houses, forcing their way in, and they will pay for nothing! I have seen these kind of men in action! These are terrible, cruel men!"

A voice of dissent rose from the back of the room. "But alcalde, our village has never had trouble from soldiers. I say we do nothing." He shrugged. "Probably they will drink and sleep. Probably they will even pay. I was a soldier for a brief time. Probably these men are just men like we are. In the morning they will leave and our coffers will be richer for their visit."

"No! You are wrong, my friend! If we do nothing, they will take what they want, destroy our village and ride away! If we fight, they will take nothing and they will not be able to ride away! We fight for our village! For our women and children! We fight for Aguafuertes!"

A cheer went up among the men, easily drowning out the few dissenters. Most of the men, especially when women were around and paying attention, fancied themselves bold rebels but up until then they had not encountered a convenient time to prove their loyalty to the revolution.

The alcalde slapped the top of the bar with his cane to regain control of the meeting. "My friends, most of the soldiers will gather here once they've seen to their mounts. Keep watch! In the afternoon, one man should be at each end of the bar. Be sure to bring your sidearms and knives. We will store rifles on a shelf beneath the bar." He motioned with his cane toward the tables that abutted the walls of the cantina. "Other men will fill the tables around the edge, at least two men at each table. Leave the tables in the center and most of the bar open for the soldiers. When they have enjoyed a drink or two and relaxed, we will take them easily!"

Again a general cheer went up. The alcalde smiled. *This will repay the son of a cur for his disrespect.*

As the men broke into smaller groups to discuss who would be seated where in the cantina later in the afternoon, the alcalde grinned. *The plan is going well. All that remains is to speak with Carmen. I will speak with her as soon as she returns from the spring. Everything will hinge on the young Capitan Guerrero being kept busy.*

His daughter would do as he asked, and his revenge would be complete. He would dishonor the young capitan in the same way the capitan's father had dishonored him.

*

Carmen truly was a classical beauty, so much so that many believed her burdened with only half the mortality the rest of them had to bear. At least she had been blessed with the complexion of the gods. She paid homage to what she considered only her very good fortune by washing her face each morning in a spring that rose from the earth. The spring was near the village, among some boulders that bore the ancient etchings from which Aguafuertes had drawn its name.

All of her life, others had regarded Carmen with a certain awe, and she was constantly rewarded with deference from males and females alike, all because of her appearance. The males fell all over themselves to please her and gain her attention, not because they entertained even the slightest notion that she would reward them

45

with anything more satisfying than a glance and a smile, but because it enabled them to enjoy a completely self-contained, wholly unrealistic fantasy for a few moments.

The females, save one or two who were as attracted to her as the boys were and for generally the same reason, simply avoided her. None would deign to actually share a young man's field of vision with her because once they'd set aside any false bravado and unrealistic comparisons, the bald truth reared its ugly head: she was simply far, far above them in a class all her own. Carmen being their admitted better, of course, did not stop the women, old and young alike, from speaking cruelly of her in small groups.

Earlier that morning, Juana, a woman old enough to be Carmen's grandmother, had watched as Carmen walked through town toward the spring. Sitting at a table on the front patio of her small house, plucking the feathers from that night's supper, she hissed, "Look at her! Her legs should look like tree trunks, walking all the way to the spring and back each morning. I heard her father will not allow mirrors in the house, so she has to go to the spring to make sure she's still prettier than everyone else."

Her daughter, Juanita, sighed. "Mama, she is not like that. I've visited with her at the spring on more than one occasion. She seldom even glances at her reflection in the water. I think she is very lonely. The men will not court her and the women are envious of her. Should we fault her for wanting to maintain what God has given her?"

"Pst! You think she's not stuck on herself? In truth she is so convinced of her own beauty that she believes even the perfect mirror of the surface of the spring is unworthy of her reflection! Someday she'll get what's coming to her. Nobody looks good forever."

Juanita looked at her mother. *When did you become so bitter?* She lifted a hand to wave in response to Carmen, who waved from the street on her way back to her house. *No tree-trunk legs there. Her legs look as good as her face.* She smiled and shook her head, wondering where that bit of envy had come from. *I will not let such bitterness creep up on me.*

*

Capitan Antonio Guerrero raised one hand and the small troop of soldiers stopped at a spring outside of Aguafuertes. He turned his horse to face them and addressed them in a voice only slightly louder than normal. "Usually I would keep half here and send half on liberty in the village, but I know many of you are anxious to return home, as am I." *Although I have nothing to return to.* Secretly, the capitan hoped to get another assignment within a few days with a new unit. He enjoyed being in the field. "We have been on the trail a long time. Therefore, we will be here probably only one night, perhaps two. Then we ride for home. Remember that you are professional soldiers, professional cavalrymen, and conduct yourselves appropriately."

*

An hour or two before the capitan and his men reached the spring, the alcalde was addressing his only daughter. "Carmen, today you will achieve your purpose in life. Today your blessed mother, rest her soul, will smile down on you from Heaven as you help your father exact revenge on the son of the pig who cursed me with this bad leg. A small troop of soldiers will arrive in town this afternoon. We will take care of the rest of them, but it's important that their leader not interfere.

"With your great beauty, you will go to the capitan. You will weaken him as only a beautiful woman can weaken a man. You will ensure that he remains... eh, *captivated* with your charms. Whatever it takes, he must not come to the cantina until I send for him, understand?"

After a brief discussion, her eyes wide with fear and anticipation and too ashamed to look anywhere but at the ground, Carmen understood all too well. She would keep the capitan occupied or she would be sent away in shame and dishonor.

*

A few hours later, soon after the soldiers had entered Aguafuertes, Carmen and her father watched as the capitan entered the small hotel. A half-hour after that, Carmen

49

approached the desk and held up a basket covered with a cloth. "*Perdón, señora...* can you tell me in which room the capitan is staying?"

The lady looked Carmen up and down and smiled. "Sí sí... he is in the back... the left corner of the courtyard."

"*Gracias, señora.*" Carmen crossed the room, opened the back door, and crossed the courtyard on a diagonal. *I do not wish to do this*, she thought. *But I must do as Papá has said. I can only hope the capitan is a gentleman and not the man Papá has made him out to be... or not a man like Papá himself.* She tapped lightly on the door with a fingernail. "*Señor?*"

No sound came from within the room.

She worked the crude wooden latch, pushed the door open a crack and stepped through. The room was steeped in shadow except for a single ray of light that shone from a window on the left onto a spot just in front of the door. She stepped into the circle of light. "*Señor?* It is Carmen Dominguez... *mi padre es el alcalde.* He... he has sent me with—"

"*Gracias, señorita*. I appreciate what your father has sent, whatever it is. Leave it there, by the door."

She stared at the figure on the bed, but was unable to make out his features. "But... but *señor*, my father...." She looked at the floor. "He sends me also."

"Do not look at the floor, *señorita*. You have nothing to be ashamed of." Something about the name Carmen tugged at his memory. *Could this be the beauty of which I heard even as far away as the capital city?* "Would you step into the light please? I mean, so the light is on your face? I have heard of a woman named Carmen who—"

As the light struck her face, she swept the hood of her cloak from her head and the capitan was struck dumb. Before him stood the most beautiful woman he'd ever seen. She was absolutely stunning, with glistening raven hair, a delicate throat, full lips, and a bronzed complexion that was smoother than a whisper on a soft breeze. Perfectly arched eyebrows and high cheekbones framed deep-set blue-green eyes.

He raised one hand, as if reaching for her

from another dimension, still uncertain whether she was real. "Please... please come closer. I will not harm you."

And in that moment, something— perhaps his spirit?—engulfed her and she felt more soothingly warm and safe than she had ever felt.

She set the basked gently on the floor, slipped her cloak from her shoulders and draped it over a post at the foot of the bed, then moved around the side of the bed as if in a trance. She reached for his hand, and in the moment they touched their souls were reunited, for they had been torn apart a very long time ago. He was the man for whom she had been waiting, even though she hadn't known. She was the woman to whom he had sworn his heart and the reason he had allowed no other women close.

She knelt alongside him, trembling, a smile playing on her lips, her eyes closed in breathless anticipation. He sat up, leaned forward, and slipped his left arm around her back, then whispered, "Welcome home, my love." They lay back on the bed together, both hungry to complete their long-awaited reunion. As their bodies strained to become the other, their souls rejoiced in having been made whole once again.

Sometime later as they lay gasping for breath, still smiling and giggling, shots rang out from somewhere outside: a lot of shots.

Antonio sprang from the bed and was scrambling into his trousers.

Carmen sat up quickly. "Oh no! No! Antonio, I'm so very sorry! I was going to tell you, but when we realized we'd found each other again it—"

Standing near the foot of the bed and tugging on a boot, he spun toward her. "Tell me what? What do you know of this?"

"My father! I... I was to keep you busy, but I didn't know! Antonio, I didn't know!"

He took a deep breath. *Her scent... her eyes... even her heartbeat.* "It's all right, Carmen. It's all right. You are the other half of my soul. Nothing can change that." He tugged on his other boot. As he reached for his gunbelt, from which his pistol and sword hung, he stumbled into the light and she had her first look at his face unencumbered by shadow.

Oh my god! He is beautiful! Perhaps more beautiful than I! Her breath caught in her throat and a curious sort of tension stretched every fiber of her being. *He is... he is the love of my life and I have betrayed him!*

Something seemed to ripple over her face and a tremor shook her heart. She looked longingly at Antonio.

But he is my love! He will forgive! Her heart twisted in her chest. *No... no, he cannot! I have betrayed him!*

Another rippling tremor shook her, and in the intensity of the moment, a crack appeared alongside her left eye and moved diagonally to the corner of her mouth. Then another ran from that one across her nose to her right eyebrow.

As she struggled with the irony of having found her love and having betrayed him all in the same moment, another crack appeared, and another, and another. Within seconds her face had shattered into rough diamonds from forehead to chin and ear to ear.

Antonio stared at her, his mouth gaping

for a moment, his eyes wide, certain he had done something to cause the anomaly. "My love, what's wrong? What happened?" Then another round of shots rang out. "Please, stay here, Carmen. I couldn't bear it if anything happened to you now." He turned and raced out of the room.

Why did he look at me like that? Carmen ran one hand over her face, then sprang from the bed, straightening her skirts and her blouse, ripped her cloak from the bedpost and stumbled out through the door. "The spring! I must get to the spring!" *I have betrayed him, and my betrayal has cost me my beauty and my love! I am so sorry, Antonio!*

*

The capitan soon realized that most of the gunfire, which was quickly abating, had come from the cantina. He burst through the door to a vision straight out of Hell. His men, who had expected no trouble and who had wanted only to relax for one night before heading home to their families, their wives and children and brothers and sisters and mothers and fathers, had been slaughtered to a man.

In slow motion, two men near the bar raised their pistols, as did another to the right side of the door.

Reaching across his body with both hands, Antonio drew his sword with his right hand and his pistol with his left hand. He cleanly severed the arm of the man to his right as he placed a neat bullet hole between the eyes of each of the two men near the bar. As men attacked him from the left and right, he fired his pistol until all the rounds were expended and four more men lay dead, then tucked it into his belt and attacked the remaining seven or eight men with his sword. A few minutes after he'd burst through the cantina door, he exited, covered in the blood of fools.

His first thought was Carmen. He raced back to the hotel and stopped at the desk where he glared at the attendant. "*Señorita* Carmen, *señora*! *Adonde esta?* Where is she?"

The woman was so frightened she couldn't speak at first. Finally she said, "The spring... outside of town, the spring!"

Antonio burst out of the hotel, climbed bareback aboard his mount and raced down the street, but when he got to the spring, Carmen wasn't there. He slipped from his horse, faced the east and cupped his hands around his mouth. "Carmen!" He faced south. "Carmen!" He called her name to the west and north as well, but received no response. Fatigue washed over him and he slumped to his knees in the sand. "Carmen... my beautiful, precious Carmen...." He raised his face to the heavens. "I have put up with much, and I have not complained, but this... this is too much." He raised his fists to the sky and roared, "Do you hear me? This is too much!"

Carmen had said her father had wanted her to keep him busy. "I will keep him busy at the end of my sword! May he rot in Hell!" He stood, gathered his horse, and rode back into town.

When he arrived, he was directed to the alcalde's home, but the alcalde wasn't there. "I think he went to his office," his maid said. "And good riddance too!" she whispered.

And of course, when Capitan Antonio

Guerrero stepped through the door of the alcalde's office, he found disappointment. The coward was slumped over his desk, still gripping a small caliber revolver with his right hand, a bullet wound in his temple.

Antonio walked out of the alcalde's office, mounted his horse, and rode south. The army would never forgive his lapse of judgment, Carmen would never forgive him for killing her father and causing that anomaly to mar her beauty, and he would never forgive himself for any of it. "I will find a cantina of my own," he mumbled. "I will find a dark corner of my own, and I will await my reckoning."

*

While Antonio was still in the cantina, Carmen made it to the spring and washed her face, but the cracks remained. "But why?" she whimpered. "I have never been vain. I wanted only to maintain what I was given. And now that I've found my love, why must I lose what has brought him to me? Why?"

Of course, there was no answer because

then, as now, the gods show up when it suits them and very seldom when they are called.

Carmen washed her face in the spring a final time, then stood. Of all the thoughts in her mind, the most prevalent was that she must disappear to wait for death, rebirth, and another chance to be with her lovely Antonio.

She wandered away from the spring, but she did not do so alone. Just as she could not have known this day would be her last day as a girl on this earth and this evening would provide her threshold to womanhood, so she could not have known that the capitan had filled her with a child.

* * *
*

THE RABBIT & THE PRIEST
A TALE FOR CHILDREN

I had gathered my grand-children, three of them, in the porch. It was story time. Rodrigo, the seven year old, said, "Grandpa, can you tell the story of the priest and the rabbit? It's my favorite, and I don't remember it all."

Carmen, who had turned eleven only a few weeks ago and who didn't visit as often as Rodrigo, said, "I'm not sure I remember that one at all, Grandfather. Anyway, this won't take too long, will it?"

Little Alicia, younger than Rodrigo by two years, just smiled.

"Certainly," I said. "And Carmen, I have a story about your namesake as well, but for today, for Rodrigo (since he spoke first) and you all, the story of the priest and the rabbit.

"The day the rabbit showed up at the south end of town was a very auspicious day indeed. It hopped, sort of, out of the scrub brush: small, gnarled mesquite, white-thorn acacia, dried-up creosote and a tuft of range grass now and then. There should have been a flower or two as well, but the lack of rain had sealed the fate of that eventuality. There had been overpowering, heavy rains to the south, but in our little corner of the world it was just hot and dry. Our fields, what few there were, had withered, and the one cow, three goats and several chickens in town had succumbed to the drought as well.

"From the time Father Rodrigo Saenz first saw the rabbit it had moved only a few meters before a crowd began to gather. Of course, bowing to good manners they remained behind the line formed by the good father's shoulders. He didn't have to raise his arms to bar their way or to establish proprietary rights over the rabbit. The rabbit had shown itself to Rodrigo first, and that was that. It was all very natural, very civilized, and only Rodrigo and the rabbit itself would dictate any further actions. The crowd itself was civilized as well, almost silent, with only the occasional murmur slipping through the dust that hung in the air.

"'Ooh, look at that!' one would say. Another would point and whisper, 'It is a rabbit!' A young one would say, 'It is beautiful!' An older one would respond with a shrug. 'It is food.' But most of us simply watched. Regardless of our comments or our silence, we all averted our gaze from the rabbit at least one time to search for other rabbits, to no avail. This rabbit was a loner.

"The rabbit seemed at once grateful for and ignorant of the crowd. It hopped, but with no great energy. The motion was more of a raising up on its hind legs and then overbalancing toward its front legs so that it had to catch itself. Certainly it was in no rush. Most rabbits hopping and grazing along a roadside, upon realizing they were being eyed by even one human, much less an increasing crowd of humans, would have done rabbit magic and disappeared, running in jagged, angled spurts. But this one didn't.

"As if on cue, someone said, 'He doesn't run. I'll bet he is deaf.' He even raised his voice slightly and called to the rabbit, 'Hey rabbit, are you deaf?' A man in the crowd snorted through his nose, then said, but quietly, just in case the rabbit was not deaf, 'Deaf or not, he must know we're here. Still he does not run.'

"And the rabbit didn't run either. After each lazy hop, it sniffed about, but in that curious, timid way that rabbits sniff, as if they don't want to be seen doing it. A man with a binocular would be hard pressed to see the nose wiggle with such a timid sniff. And having sniffed, if there were anything nearby that seemed succulent, the rabbit would nibble, again very timidly. All of this as the town slowly emptied and the crowd across the street grew around old Saenz.

"Nobody had thought to ask Rodrigo Saenz why he hadn't picked up a rock and brained that poor rabbit. It would create a fine stew and there would be enough leftover rabbit for a few meals besides. It was a good thing to be a man of peace, a man of the cloth, but all men need food regardless of their calling, and nobody in the town had eaten for a few days.

"Truth be known, Rodrigo probably had gone longer without food than the others. He was the village priest, and a good one. By that I mean he always set the good example and provided for others before he provided for himself. But the fact remained that he hadn't provided a dead, cleaned rabbit for anyone. In a moment of weakness, I thought, *How dare he not take this opportunity to feed his flock?*

"As if giving thanks for that thought and expressing it as action, the rabbit hopped, sniffed, nibbled.

"Well, as an elder in the town, it is among my responsibilities to question the priest when necessary. I was standing behind Rodrigo and to his right, and I tugged lightly on his sleeve. Barely above a whisper, I said, 'Rodrigo?' He inclined his head toward me slightly but kept his attention on the rabbit. I said, 'Rodrigo, should we not give thanks for this bounty and thump it on the head with a rock?' Imperceptibly to anyone but me, he shook his head, then said, 'No.'

"The rabbit hopped and sniffed and tasted a bit of discarded baling wire that must have reminded him of red grass. Not too intelligent, our rabbit."

Carmen giggled.

I said to the padre, 'I'm sure any of us could outrun it and put it out of its misery.

Old Garcia has his cane,' I said. I could borrow it and—' But he interrupted me, again with a simple 'No.' I tried to explain. I said, 'Rodrigo, I think it might be no great loss to rabbits who know what they're about. Perhaps this one is an outcast.' But the good priest just smiled and said, 'No. He is not an outcast. He is an example.'

"The rabbit hopped and sniffed, then leaned into another hop. 'An example?' I said. 'An example of what?'

"The priest turned to me. Very quietly, he said, 'Gervasio, the rabbit is a miracle. I'm not sure how I know, but he is a miracle and an example.' Then he said one of the simplest and most important things I've ever heard: 'Listen... he is speaking to us.' Then he turned slightly and repeated it for the crowd. 'All of you,' he said, 'be still and listen closely... he is speaking to us all.'

"Well, as you might imagine, there were more murmurs from the crowd than before, and all at one time. They almost reached the point of being a little loud, but then they died as quickly as they had begun. As the priest had suggested, we watched and we listened.

"The rabbit hopped, sniffed, and nibbled, hopped, sniffed and nibbled. It was a slow process, but somehow he held our attention. As the rabbit hopped, sniffed and nibbled, we and the priest shuffled along with him. As we neared the center of town, the earth rumbled, then calmed, but even the earth moving beneath our feet seemed of less importance than watching the rabbit, listening to the rabbit. The rabbit hopped, sniffed, and nibbled, we listened, and after a time we came to understand."

Little Rodrigo Saenz Rodriguez Arrancado turned his face up to look at me, his eyes wide. "What did you understand, Grandfather?"

I sipped my coffee, then set the cup on the table beside my chair. "An old lesson that presents itself in many ways many times during a life, perhaps to keep us on track—that things are very seldom as they seem."

Carmen smiled, having recently come into the certainty that there is nothing she doesn't know, and was seemingly wary of a trap. "But a rabbit is still only a rabbit, Grandfather."

"Oh yes, yes... it was still a rabbit, true enough, but as the priest said, it was a great deal more than a rabbit. Tell me, Carmen, Rodrigo, Alicia... do you believe in angels?"

Rodrigo and his younger sister nodded, their eyes wide with anticipation.

Carmen crossed her arms in what some might have thought was defiance, but it was not defiance. It was derision. "Of *course*, Grandfather. Things that exist are not dependent on belief."

"Exactly. Also, some things are more than just one thing. The rabbit—" I swept my gaze over all of them. "The rabbit was an angel."

As the other two stared, still wide eyed, Carmen almost allowed her jaw to drop open before she caught herself. "Now *that* would be a matter for belief, that one real thing could also be another. Did you say the rabbit spoke?"

I nodded. "The priest, Rodrigo Saenz, said the rabbit was speaking to us. We heard no actual words—at least I didn't—but that one statement and the possibilities it created caused us to listen. And that was what mattered... that we listened. But let me get back to the story. Then you too will under-stand."

All three were staring at me with rapt attention.

"We continued to watch the rabbit as it hopped and sniffed and then either nibbled or, if there was nothing to nibble, hopped again. It seemed unaware of us, or at least unconcerned. And that is how it spoke to us. Rabbits are very rational people. Human beings are not. But that day, the rabbit taught the humans what it means to be rational.

"There were no words that I heard, but there were impressions, sensations, that meant the same as words but bigger. They came into my mind as clearly and with as much meaning as if spoken to me personally in an otherwise quiet room."

Carmen frowned. "But what did it say? For example, did it say," and here she paused and put on a faux baritone voice, "'I am an angel, so you must not eat me! You must be still and ignore your grumbling belly as I lecture you!'" Her smile broadened. "Did it say that?"

I looked calmly at her, and I spoke softly. "No, Carmen... no, that the rabbit was an angel is my own conclusion. But the impressions that washed over me, although clear as speech, were not separate and disjointed. They were smoother even than the smoothest rhetoric I've heard uttered by humans. And the impressions overlapped in waves. Unfortunately, I can describe them only with speech, so the description will lack much of the substance.

"The first impression was that the rabbit was at peace. It meant no harm and experienced no fear. It was not separate of us, but part of us, or rather we were part of it. Had there been a thick field of lettuce that he knew was ours growing alongside the road, he would not have partaken, except perhaps of a head that had grown wild, its seeds removed from the field by a breeze.

"The second impression was that it knew we could kill it and eat it but that we wouldn't. There were three dozens of us plus some, the whole town. And there's the wisdom—we could easily have destroyed the rabbit, but only a few could have eaten.

Collectively we did not want to know which few would have eaten and what they would have done to fend off the rest of us.

"The third impression was that where there is life and reason, hope is eternal. The rabbit, left alive, hopped and sniffed, hoping to find minuscule morsels of food. The bits of food he found seemed only enough to fuel the next hop to the next morsel.

"And that brought the fourth impression, the collective realization that we were rooting for the rabbit, and therefore rooting for ourselves. And in that way, the rabbit moved the entire two kilometers through the town: hopping, sniffing, and nibbling when there was something to nibble."

"And you all just moved along with him?"

I nodded. "We all just moved along with him, even through the trembling that occurred as he reached the center of town."

"And he continued to hop and nibble and pay no attention?"

"He continued to hop and nibble and pay no attention, either to the trembling earth or to us, his faithful audience."

"And when he reached the end of town?"

"Ahh... when he reached the north end of town—and remember, this had been an arduous journey of several hours—for the first time he stopped without sniffing or nibbling. He turned to his left, perpendicular to the road, sat back on his haunches—I had never seen a rabbit do something like that before—and looked at us. Something... a very strong kindness, I think, like a blessing... washed over us all, and there was the deep-throated sound of a truck engine from back the way we had all come, we and the rabbit together.

"Of course, we turned our heads and looked south. There was a large farm truck, its sideboards straining. That's when our priest, Rodrigo Saenz, the man who was wise enough to have us listen, said, 'Look!' It was the most excitement he had shown in contemporary memory."

"We turned back to him and looked in the direction he was pointing. The rabbit was gone. We looked farther along the road, but it was not there. We looked into the desert on that side of the road, but there was no trace. Some, I included, even turned to look behind us, thinking perhaps the rabbit might have raced past us as we were distracted by the truck, but it was not there either." I shrugged. "It had simply disappeared. But stranger yet, nobody asked anyone else about it or questioned it. Everyone was calm and smiling. And that was the final impression: the rabbit was gone, but it was all right that the rabbit was gone.

"We turned our attention back to the truck and it had passed the center of the village. We began walking in that direction. When he noticed we were coming toward him, the driver of the truck applied the brakes, which squealed and pulled the truck to a stop. Dust almost obliterated our view for a moment, but it cleared soon enough. The truck was overloaded with crates of chickens and produce, and standing in the very front, just behind the cab, was a milk cow.

"As the driver and his assistant climbed down to greet us, our priest stepped forward. 'To what do we owe the honor of your visit?' he said, still smiling. 'Has the rabbit sent you?'

"The driver stared at Rodrigo for a moment, then took off his cap, looked at the ground and shook his head. Then he looked back up at the priest. 'Strangest thing I've ever seen, Padre,' he said. I'll never forget the look on his face. I'm paraphrasing now, of course, but he said something like, 'Down south... Agua Rocosa, they'd heard you were running out of food.' He indicated his friend and himself, and said, 'We were tasked with bringing food to your village. Well, some fifty kilometers south of here, the narrow road over the mountains had washed out. Probably that last big rain a month ago. I understand you folks haven't had any problem with rain.' He smiled a bit at his own joke.

"Then he said he set the parking brake and he an' José—that was his assistant's name—got out of the truck to look at the washout. Well, they couldn't believe their eyes. The gap was three or four meters across and several meters deep. He said there wasn't enough loose material around to fill it, not with just the two of them and no equipment to speak of. He and José decided there was nothing they could do, so they climbed back into the truck and began the frightening process of backing down the mountain.

"He said they'd gone almost a kilometer backing down that narrow, winding road when José spotted a small rabbit in the road behind the truck. He told the driver to stop, that there was something magical about the rabbit. The driver said he thought maybe José was crazy, but he stopped anyway to humor him.

"Ahh, but when they got out of the truck and looked, the rabbit was gone. On their way back to the truck he was teasing José about his overactive imagination. And just as they were about to get back in the truck, the ground shook hard all over. A great cloud of dust rose ahead of them. The driver said, 'For some reason, I looked at José. He was calm. He told me the road ahead was clear now.'

"So the truck driver and his assistant got back in the truck and drove forward. When they again approached the gap in the road, they could tell where it had been, but it was mostly filled. They got out and inspected it to be sure they could trust their own eyes, then got back in the truck and drove across it.

"And that is the story of the priest, my friend Rodrigo Saenz, and the rabbit who was an angel."

Carmen just stared for a long moment, then got up and hugged my neck. "Grandfather, did you say there was a story about a woman named Carmen also? Is it magical too? May I visit more often?"

I laughed with the joy that only a child—or an angel—can provide. "There is at least one story about the beautiful woman named Carmen, and perhaps more than one. It is indeed magical, as are all events that matter, and you may visit, my beloved granddaughter, anytime you like. But now it's time for all of you to get some rest."

I stood and accompanied them into the house and down the hallway to their rooms.

* * *
*

THE DAWN OF RIGOBERTO

The men had just struggled ashore from their boats and were looking forward to joining their women and children in their homes, from which soft lights were beginning to emanate as the sun gave up the day. As a few were busily stowing what must be stowed, most were emptying the hold of the day's catch, creating a new reality for the fish they'd caught, who were becoming the vendors' concern. As the fish made the transition from captives to wares, the vendors variously cleaned and iced and chopped and salted them in preparation for the next morning's sales.

A very small wooden shack, grey with decades of weathering and salt spray, was situated just across the dock from the largest boat. As an occasional gust of wind blew in from the sea, the old door slapped the side of the shack, its hinges complaining loudly, then pushed itself a few inches away from the wall as if spurning an unwanted lover. Then it hesitated as if fickle before slapping the side of the shack with less anger.

It was not only the end of another long day, but the end of the month. Inside the shack, Rigoberto, the captain of the largest boat, was doling out his crewmembers' wages plus a modest bonus for the excellent catch. He was the largest man in town, easily standing a head taller than all others, and the handsomest, with a look that was born of the sea and his father, whom, to his knowledge, he had never met: Rigoberto was weathered but not worn, ageless but not aged. His physical prowess and temper were unmatched.

Everyone took note of the former, of course—the women as in a dream state and the men enviously—but fortunately very few had encountered the latter, as the kindness and respect with which he treated those within his charge also was unmatched. When the last of his crewmembers had left for home, Rigoberto stepped around the table and through the door, then closed the door securely and latched it with a small piece of wood hinged on a nail. He glanced over his boat a final time, giving his livelihood its due, then turned for home.

As Rigoberto strode up the wide dirt street, he glanced up at *La Montaña de Sueños Cautivos*, The Mountain of Captive Dreams. The mountain captured not only the dreams of the villagers, nesting them and nurturing them and then allowing them to seep back down to the village when they were sorely needed, but also the imagination of any who believed in legends, as most in the sleepy village did. Rigoberto believed more than most, and for a much stronger reason than the wealth of dreams stored there. Rigoberto's mother had wandered off to the mountain within a few weeks of his birth.

His uncle, who had raised him, had been swept overboard and lost the previous year, and his aunt had died along with her new son in childbirth some twenty years earlier, so his mother, if she were alive on the mountain, was his only living relative. The mountain was his touchstone.

*

The villagers had sensed that the woman who had given birth to Rigoberto was different, especially as they witnessed the speed with which he grew physically and intellectually. Many had thought—secretly, of course, for it wasn't prudent to be less than secretive about such things—that she was a witch and perhaps even a consort to the sea itself. Indeed, when a generation had come and gone since she'd wandered away, she had grown in the minds of many from witch to goddess.

The villagers shook their fists and issued stern warnings (while keeping one wary eye on the mountain, of course) when inclement weather lasted longer than they considered natural or when lightning strikes came closer than was comfortable, and they offered up loud prayers of allegedly never-ending gratitude when the fleet returned with their holds full of fish or when the rains came when they were welcome or stopped when they were not. Thus had Rigoberto's mother garnered a great deal more responsibility than she ever would have wanted.

*

As he glanced up at *La Montaña de*

Sueños Cautivos, in a clearing near the peak he detected the hint of a creature, descending slowly. He continued along the dusty street, but averted his gaze and frowned. *The mountain has always been densely covered with jungle; there are no clearings.*

When he was twelve he'd been to the top once with his uncle, "To see the home of the ancient and future king," his uncle had said, but he was certain the man had hoped to find his sister, Rigoberto's mother. The trek had taken them the better part of a day. They had followed a stream that the father of the future king himself had followed when he had thought to separate himself from the world. Rigoberto thought, *That he wasn't successful in secluding himself was a good thing.* Everyone in the village had heard the story. Had the man not eventually been overcome with loneliness and come down from the mountain, he would never have met the mother of the future king, and the king himself would still be waiting in the ether for an appropriate set of parents.

Rigoberto had expected a castle, or at the very least a large dwelling (and in a back corner of his mind, he secretly hoped they would find his mother), but when he and his uncle had arrived at the top, the king's home was little more than a cave with a pool nearby. And of course, his mother was nowhere to be seen.

Rigoberto had looked up at his uncle, disappointment evident in his face. "But there is no throne, Tio. How can a king rule with no throne?"

"Ah but there is, my son," his uncle had said. "The throne is a holy circle, and it's on the roof. Only the king can see it, and only the king, when he's seated in its exact center, is given a view all the way to that horizon where imagination folds into reality. He knows and commands earth, wind, fire and sea. Thus is his wisdom multiplied and his subjects prosper in peace."

"And no others could employ the same vision?" Rigoberto asked, for he already had heard the whispered rumors in town concerning his mother.

"No, she couldn't—I mean, no... only the king would be given such vision."

*

As he walked, Rigoberto glanced at the mountain again. It was a solid green canopy. The clearing he thought he'd seen only seconds earlier and its occupant were gone, a figment of his imagination dusted away on the light breeze coming in from the sea. Then, just as he started to avert his gaze again, *There!* Just over halfway down the mountain, the same creature he'd seen near the top had appeared again. *No doubt in another clearing that doesn't exist*, he thought, then smiled and shook his head. *It has been a very long day.* But before he looked away this time, he glanced quickly again and saw that the creature was actually a crone, bent at the shoulders and perhaps leaning on a walking stick as she made her way down the mountain.

The rhythm of his heart seemed to double as he considered the possibilities. Then his thoughts shifted from the crone to the speed with which she was descending. If she were the same creature he'd seen in the clearing near the top, she had descended well over a thousand feet in less than a minute. *Very swiftly*, he thought, a bit surprised. And his thoughts shifted yet again, from his mother to the goddess of the rumors, just as if he were certain in his soul—or perhaps merely hopeful—that they were two different beings. He glanced up again to confirm his suspicion, but the clearing was gone. He sighed as his anxiety waned. *A long day, but a good day.* He turned left at the corner and continued toward his home.

It was an auspicious day.

*

Rigoberto had opened a few cans of whatever he thought might combine well, poured them into a single stew pan and set them atop a very low fire to let the various flavors work out the details. He had settled into his favorite chair when a thought came to him from the outside in, as if he were eavesdropping. *I'm telling you, it's time.*

Time for what? he thought, then said, "Time for what?" When he suddenly realized he was talking to himself he shook his head and grinned. *Time for a vacation, perhaps.*

The sea sent a breeze to rattle the seaward

shutters as another thought occurred, slightly more intense this time, as a thought cannot be characterized as louder or quieter. *He has reached his thirty-third anniversary. It is time.*

As if he had no choice, Rigoberto thought, *He? Who is he?* A strange sensation of being on the precipice of knowledge trembled through him and he looked about the room. He murmured, "Am... am I he?" Of course, he was alone in the room and immediately felt foolish.

It is time. You must come to know your father.

The shutters rattled again, and Rigoberto stood, turning frantically this way and that. "*Me? My* father? Who are you? How do you know—"

Be calm, my son. All is well. Be calm and you will know. Be calm.... Be calm....

A sweet aroma wafted through the room, reminding Rigoberto of the stew. He went into the kitchen, welcoming the normalcy of the action as a catalyst to reattach himself to reality while regaining control of his senses. A moment later, as he removed the pan from the fire and set out *two* bowls and *two* spoons, an eerie calm settled over him. *She's right... all is well. We will share a meal... and I will meet my father.*

The shutters on the seaward side of the house rattled again, lightly, as if with glee, but Rigoberto was moving toward the front of the room. Just as he got there a knock sounded. He opened the door and his arms. "*Tierra... mi madre, Tierra....*"

A small woman, bent at the shoulders, nodded. "*Mi hijo*... my son....."

He smiled and gathered her into his arms, gently. "*Mama, tu eres mi corazón.* You are my heart."

"*Oh sí.*" She smiled up at him, pinched his cheek and leaned her walking stick against the wall near the door. They went to the small table, where they shared a meal of stew and dark bread.

*

Some time later, on their way to the shore, she said, "Having enticed the sea and become with child, I ascended to await the king to beg his forgiveness and receive guidance. I was allowed to watch over you, but as penance it was always from that place where horizons converge. Today you receive your birthright... today, again I become only memory."

On a massive rock just northwest of the village, she smiled and hugged Rigoberto, then turned away and raised her hands over the sea. "*Neptuno*, behold your son, of earth and sea!"

As a great spiraling wave rose up, rapturous ripples wafted through Rigoberto, each filling him with more strength, power and wisdom. The spiral engulfed the rock upon which he and his mother were standing, and they began to spin. Rising they spun more and more tightly until Tierra blinked out of existence and everything flashed to a stop.

Rigoberto awoke on his back on the beach. He looked about. Nobody else was there, but he sensed he was not alone. He sifted a bit of earth through his fingers. Then he rose, stretched one hand toward the sea and watched as the whitecaps became smooth. He smiled, turned and walked back to the village, his sea-green eyes reflecting creation itself.

* * *
*

THE STORYTELLER

The cantina in Agua Rocosa was the usual thick-walled adobe building, dimly lighted through small, deep, open windows on three sides. There was one window on either side of the only door, which opened to the east, and two on each wall that raced away from that wall toward the bar, a heavy wooden affair topped with burnished mesquite. It ran along much of the west wall, and to the north end of it a single wooden door with a simple wooden latch opened into small back room. The proprietor and bartender, Juan-Carlos Salazár, used the back room for storage and his wife, Ofelia, sometimes used it as a makeshift office.

There was no rear exit from the cantina, except one that might be used in times of dire emergency by persons much smaller than Juan-Carlos. That exit had begun as a small drainage hole near the back corner of the storage room, but according to Juan-Carlos, a certain older gentleman from a nearby village had engaged a few delinquent youngsters to enlarge it over a period of a month or two, enough so that a thin shouldered boy of thirteen or so could successfully wriggle through and procure an occasional bottle of tequila for a five-finger discount. The boy and the bottle would disappear back to the home of the old gentleman, where both of them would be paid handsomely: the boy with a few coins, and the old gentleman with the finest tequila he could procure at no cost.

Juan-Carlos would put his hands in the air. "What can I do?" he would say more often than necessary to his most trusted paying customers. "The old gentleman really is harmless and he takes a bottle only every month or thereabouts. Oh, and did you know his woman is a witch?" For no reason at all he crossed himself and wiped at an imaginary stain on the bar with a rag in which the creases were permanent and that had stiffened with the soiled oil of his hands as the moisture had siphoned from it during repeated use. "Certainly I shouldn't deny the harmless old gentleman his pleasure, which he derives not only from drinking my tequila but also, perhaps even more so, from the manner in which it is obtained." He paused, put the back of his hand alongside his mouth and leaned toward the two men on the other side of the bar. "Although he could well afford to purchase it from me or even open his own cantina and stock it with much better spirits than I have ever been able to serve here." Catching a signal in his peripheral vision, he glanced down the bar, then yelled over his shoulder, "Ofelia, can you come help with the bar?" There was no response. He turned back to his attentive audience. "I'll be back in a moment to continue the story, if you will excuse me." He wandered off to pour a glass for the customer who had motioned for him, then sat the bottle on the bar so he would not be interrupted so soon again.

While he was gone, Javier, a young *vaquero* from a horse ranch just up the coast, nudged the young gringo standing next to him at the bar and grinned. "It's a very good thing that Juan-Carlos is given to storytelling. Otherwise he might have to admit to drinking his profits himself."

The other man was not from Agua Rocosa. He was a *norteamericano* who had come in on the bus that morning. The day was so hot that even in his khaki trousers, slip-on loafers and white linen shirt, he had parched instantly. Even before coming into the cantina for some quick relief, he had felt compelled to stay in the village for a few days. Once the cool Negra Modelo had crossed his lips, he'd discovered two things: that few things are better than the luxury of a Negra Modelo and lime on a scalding hot day, and that the business he had come to conduct farther to the south suddenly wasn't nearly as important as sitting in this bar enjoying himself with his new *compañeros*. He looked at Javier, his eyes wide. "Do you really think so?"

Javier simply stared at him for a moment, then slapped him on the back and broke into raucous laughter. "Do I *think* so?" As Juan-Carlos was on his way back, he leaned closer. "For a moment I didn't realize you were joking, *mi amigo*. But of course, you smelled his pickled-worm breath for yourself." Still grinning, he shook his head.

"Do I think so...."

Juan-Carlos saw that the two men were talking and passed them by to attend to customers at a few tables on the floor.

Javier poured himself another shot of tequila and downed it, then took a swig of his Leon. *"Como se llama, mi amigo nuevo?* What's your name, my new friend?"

The young man straightened and offered his hand. "Oh, I'm Charlie... Charlie Task."

"Oh sí... Carlos... Charlie." Javier nodded. "It's a good name."

"So... what about the drainage in the back? I mean, the hole... the drainage hole. Why would the boys expand it if they weren't coming in to procure tequila for their elderly friend?"

Javier looked at him for a long moment, then shrugged and sipped his beer. "Who knows? Perhaps it was not boys at all." He waved one hand vaguely about. "This is a very old establishment. Perhaps the sun, parched and dry as it must be, enlarged the hole a bit to gain entry to some refreshment. Perhaps the wind, blowing as it does constantly, became thirsty in its passing. It

93

passes right by here, you know. Surely all that tequila must be an attractive nuisance. Perhaps even the water itself, when it rains or when a big storm comes from the sea, was jealous of the bottled nectar." He shrugged. "Perhaps all three conspired to enlarge the hole, the sun and wind in hopes of quenching their thirst and the water hoping to blend the nectar of the agave plant with the heady flavors of the sea."

Charlie was rapt with attention, though he occasionally glanced past Javier's shoulder to track the bartender's progress.

Javier continued, motioning with his cerveza. "I have heard of that process—the sun and the wind and the water combining to wear down even large, heavy fortifications —although I have never seen it in action myself. I think it would take a while longer than I can spare to watch, and I don't know that I would want to witness its secrets anyway. It sounds something like magic to me. But if they could do that—if the wind, water and sun could conspire to wear down even a strong fortress to low, crumbled ruins—how much less difficult would it be for them to enlarge a hole where there shouldn't have been one in the first place? Not too hard, I think." He shrugged again, then laughed. "And maybe it was the boys after all... maybe they did it for the old gentleman, or maybe for themselves. I think it doesn't matter." He gestured with his drink toward the bartender. "For Juan-Carlos, it is enough that the story exists and that he is blessed to tell it. I promise you, he cares more about stories and their telling than he cares even for his own tequila. And for me, it matters only as an enjoyable way to pass the time on a hot day with a cold cerveza." He poured and drained another shot of tequila, then took another swig of his beer.

Charlie raised his Negra Modelo. "To the stories then."

Javier grinned as his Leon bottle clinked against Charlie's Negra Modelo. "*A las historias y nuevos amigos.* To the stories and new friends."

Juan-Carlos was back with a tray full of empty bottles and a few glasses. He moved past the two men as they toasted, set the tray on the bar, then dipped two empty glasses behind the bar into a container of tepid water, upon the surface of which a soap rainbow was floating. He withdrew them and dipped them into the next container, this one of rinse water, upon the surface of which were the beginnings of its own rainbow. It is well known in certain circles that glass is a conductor of magic from one place to another, especially for rainbows and other visual effects. He set the glasses on a relatively clean bar towel and looked up. "That sounds like an excellent toast: to the stories, was it?"

Javier nodded. "*Sí, sí. A las historias, a nuevos amigos, y al narrador.* For without the storyteller, the stories would not be told." He raised his bottle toward Juan-Carlos and nodded.

Juan-Carlos quickly dunked two more glasses, rinsed them and set them on the towel. He dried his hands on the large dirty spot on his otherwise white apron. "That earns you a cerveza on the house, my friend." He grinned, reached into the large cooler beneath the bar and withdrew two Leons. He opened both and sat one in front of Javier, then raised the other. "*Gracias, mi amigo.*" He glanced at Charlie. "*Y tu, mi amigo.* When you believe you are ready for another Negra Modelo, it's on me. And speaking of the stories, do you remember where I left off?"

Javier shrugged. "It was a good story, but I don't remember."

Charlie snapped his fingers. "The old gentleman... you were just saying, in strictest confidence of course, that if he wanted to, the old gentleman could even open his own cantina."

Juan-Carlos nodded. "That's right. He certainly has plenty of money, judging by the way he goes around in the finest suits and his woman always in the latest fashions." He sighed, then lowered his voice and leaned closer to his audience of two. "And you know, nobody knows or remembers where the old gentleman attained such wealth... or else they have forgotten as a matter of convenience." He reached to wipe at the same imaginary spot he'd eradicated earlier. "Anyway, I think perhaps enduring the relatively minor inconvenience of 'misplacing' a bottle of tequila every couple of weeks is preferable to denying the old gentleman his pleasure—did I mention that his woman is a witch?"

He paused and crossed himself, then spread his arms, palms out, the stiff rag still dangling from one hand. "What if I filled in that drainage hole all at one time and then discover one morning that the contents of all my casks and bottles have magically spoiled, having received the full blunt of a spell or curse? How would that be good for what little business I have in my poor cantina?" He wiped the spot on the bar again. "I tell you, it would be no good at all." He tapped his temple with one finger. "We thinking men must consider everything—not only our business and how to keep it, but how to avoid upsetting any witches or supernatural beings who might be about."

Upon hearing the words "supernatural beings" a few other locals sidled up alongside the young vaquero and the gringo, who had endured the best telling up to that time of what would eventually come to be known among the town's jokesters as "The Tale of the Disappearing Tequila."

Since an audience had gathered, Juan-Carlos lined up glasses and set two bottles of tequila on the bar. This was the really good stuff so, being a thinking man, he announced with a grandiose swing of his arms, "After each of you have only six drinks—no no, only five—the rest are half price!" Everyone applauded his generosity, even though many realized none of them probably would make it past four drinks of the potent worm-driven stuff, much less five. Still, they were courteous and would allow him his moment of false generosity, if only to prove they were more generous than he.

With that, the bartender swung his arms wide in a gesture of welcome. "I have a story for you—perhaps the greatest story ever told in Agua Rocosa—about a man who, having never been seen in the region before, suddenly rose up from the mud plain just to the north of town." He lay one hand over the center of his chest. "And I was honored and humbled to be among the small crowd who witnessed his emergence first hand that day." He paused and looked along the line of attentive listeners, then wagged one index finger in the air. "Ah... but first you must hear about the rain."

The gringo Charlie, not wanting to make waves as the newest friend at the bar, only donned a slight frown of the kind that might appear on the face of a man who believes he is being bamboozled, but next to him, Javier said, "But the man who rose from the mud... let's have that one first." A few of the other men along the bar murmured their approval.

Juan-Carlos slung his towel over his shoulder and shook his head slightly, as if about to address a wayward child. Again he scanned the line of men at the bar. "My friends, I am the storyteller, charged by all of you and even nature itself to record and convey the stories. The arrival of the man of mud is perhaps the most important event that ever happened in Agua Rocosa." He shrugged. "As such, and as the responsibility for the stories falls to me, I believe the story of the man of mud is deserving of a solid foundation on which it can stand, proudly showcased."

He looked at Javier again and his voice grew quiet, although still loud enough for the other men to hear, especially since they were leaning forward and breathing silently, without disturbing the air. "It is part of the craft of the storyteller to know that some-times... sometimes, my friends... the stories swirl in together, like tears and laughter stirred into cream. Sometimes they are even lost altogether in the swirl.

"But we are fortunate today, for these stories, the ones I'm about to tell and the story of the man of mud, stack one upon the other, building in importance. In time I will say the story about the mud man, but first I must lay the foundation." Again he lay one hand over the center of his chest. "It is my duty."

Charlie smiled, took a long swig of his beer and settled his mind for the coming story.

Juan-Carlos said, "My friends, you are here for a story. This is the tale of the wind and the rain, odd bird behavior and the boarding house."

A few of the men, including Javier, nodded their tacit approval.

"Several decades ago, back when I was only a very small boy and you were not even a glimmer of lust in your father's eyes, on an otherwise beautiful morning, an over-powering sense of grief washed ashore from the sea and covered the land. The skies, angered at having witnessed the involuntary influx of such sorrow, turned grey and then brown and then suddenly very dark. My friends, this was not the usual darkness of low, dark clouds stretching to all the horizons, but a special kind of strong darkness, with a tired, melancholy sadness and even anger about it.

"As we humans tried to get out of bed in the morning, we slogged through the weary oppression seeping from those skies, seeming almost to have to swim up from sleep, even though it hadn't begun raining yet. Still, the gloom permeated all of the air, and it almost forced even the youngest, most carefree among us back beneath the covers.

"For days the massive clouds rippled and boiled like black chili simmering over a low fire for a very long time. The cattle and horses lay in the field and in the stalls, listless, and even the snails and mud turtles withdrew into the dark confines of their houses, which certainly must have contained a less-despondent air than was outside. The cacti and other plants, even the trees, sagged as if filled with despair.

"And it wasn't only the actors on the stage whose spirit waned, but the spirit of the stage itself. Those low, dark clouds grumbled among themselves, as if debating whether to scour the whole area and be done with it or, perhaps, to withhold the replenishment of water from the sea itself in retaliation for the grief it had brought to the land. The sun, embarrassed with its inability to push away the sadness and suddenly caught up in its own ego, crossed its arms and sat back, pretending it was in charge.

"I listened closely in those days, eager as I was to learn all I could, and I swear I heard the sun announce that it would refuse to break the clouds' blockade from one day to the next, just as if that's what it truly wanted." Juan-Carlos leaned forward over the bar. "At least that's what it sounded like it said. With its usually bright, cheery voice saddened and muffled by the clouds, it was difficult to be sure."

He sighed and straightened. "In any case, we never saw even the glimmer of an attempt on its part to penetrate the clouds or the gloom that filled the world beneath them. Of course, as you might imagine if you've ever been embarrassed with a failure while trying to impress someone, any attempt that failed would have served only to prove that it was not up to the task.

"And the wind...." He flung his bar towel over his shoulder and sighed. "Ah, the wind.... Well, you all know it has traced the same route since the beginning of time, rushing from the sea to the mountains in the morning and from the mountains back to the sea in the evening.

"But for the first time in eternity it seemed confused about which direction to go, perhaps because with the overcast there was so little difference between morning and evening, and even between day and night. Instead of rushing along in the dark, the wind loitered timidly among the rocks and trees, afraid to rush off confidently in one direction for fear it might plunge off the very earth itself and be lost. Scraping around among the rocks and trees, all of whom were also variously sad or angry or, at the least, confused and wondering what was going on, it manufactured a sorrowful sound, as if worrying aloud at the possibility of being trapped among those rocks and trees forever.

"And you know, some of it *was* trapped there even when that dreadful week ended. To this day, when you walk among the rocks and trees on the lower slopes of the mountains above the village, you will hear remnants of that frightened windsong and feel nervous bits of it tugging at the cuffs of your trousers and the sleeves of your shirt."

He shook his head again. "It was a dark, troubled time. And then, on the evening of the first day, having apparently decided to wash the grief from the air with electricity and rinse it with water, the black, roiling clouds released lightning bolts that seemed to split the very heavens. The thunder was such that it sent even the most vicious dogs into hiding, and then came a torrent of rain.

But it was a very unusual torrent. It was composed of the massive raindrops that you see in a sudden, short-lived downpour, the sort that occurs when a gigantic container that has the appearance of a cloud but carries far more liquid than any cloud could carry suddenly bursts and drops the entire load all at one time and all in one place.

You know the kind of downpour I mean: perhaps it lasts only a half-hour and is soaked immediately into the thirsty earth, yet it drowns even frogs and fish in its passing. Like the raindrops in that kind of downpour, the smaller of these raindrops were an inch across and most were much larger. And it began all at once—again, as in the kind of downpour with which we're all familiar—but it kept coming and coming and coming for the whole week. And instead of falling all in one place, it fell everywhere.

"Now, as you might well imagine from the size of those drops, there was very little space between them, and they cleared the skies completely of birds and bats and flying insects within moments after the rain began. The larger birds—say generally anything larger than a kestrel—that needed to get from one place to another simply walked. They held their wings aloft in a kind of umbrella, and no doubt they wore a visage of disgust that only a bird, with its fixed beak and those little beady eyes, could express.

"The smaller birds—all kinds of sparrows and wrens and even the smaller owls—found a place to hide and latched on for fear of being washed away. And the bats... well, we all know they stayed safe and dry in the upper reaches of wherever they were hanging when the rain began. Well, after a long week of that kind of rain—"

"What about the insects?" The question had come in the scratchy voice of the thin, bespectacled Ernesto at the end of the bar.

Juan-Carlos looked at him. "*¿Que?*"

Ernesto's Adam's apple bobbed. "The insects—what about them?" At 5'7" Ernesto weighed less than 110 pounds. His eyes appeared to bulge behind the thick glasses balanced on his thin, hooked nose. His leathery skin might have been stretched over his narrow chin and his high, sharp cheek-bones. That plus his thin, long, antennae-like moustache and his spindly arms and legs perhaps belied a greater than usual appreciation for our six-legged friends. "You said the larger birds scowled and stomped through the streets, and that the smaller birds and the bats remained hidden, but what about the insects?"

Juan-Carlos nodded. "Ah, of course, of course. *Gracias, Ernesto.*" He turned back to the others. "Yes, yes, the insects... my friends, I can tell you there were no bugs—no insects—anywhere: none flying in the air, none crawling or hopping along on the ground or in the trees, not even grass-hoppers jumping on screen doors to annoy the people in their houses." He shrugged. "If I had to make excuses for them, I would say they didn't want to run the risk of encoun-tering those angry, larger birds who were stomping about the village looking for something on which they could take out their frustration and their sore feet."

The small group of men joined Juan-Carlos in healthy laughter for a moment. When it died down, he resumed the serious tone with which he'd conveyed the earlier part of the story. "And so it went, the rain coming down in sheets, twenty-four hours a day without a single break for a solid week.

"Well, in that week alone, the few trees we have in the village and the surrounding area, having shaken off their despondency with the coming of the rain, grew an average of two feet, and those few folks who had the foresight to plant a few seeds saw the plants sprout, come to majority, produce vegetables and die off. All in that one week!

"I mentioned earlier that I was only a child, but I would bet those people and those in their good graces ate very well for the next month or so."

A couple of the men snickered and shook their heads, to which Juan-Carlos raised both hands.

"I know, I know... this story is less believable than most of the tales you hear in my poor little cantina, but consider, I do not charge a fee. I tell them only because they must be told."

He topped off a few of the men's glasses and set a couple more beers on the bar. "At any rate, I am too honest to ask you to believe me. When you travel again to the capital, you can check the records for yourself. Botanists and other agriculture types came from the university to study the phenomenon, and they took their recorded results back to the capital." A glimmer crept into his eyes. "And many of them stayed right here in the village."

José, who owned a small fishing fleet and usually sat alone at a table in the back corner of the cantina to conduct his business, was sitting at the bar on the end opposite Ernesto. He took the bait. "Who did they stay with? Maybe those who put them up could fill in more of the story."

Juan-Carlos wiped the imaginary spot on the bar again. "Yes, yes... let's see.... Do any of you remember the small lodging house just at the north end of the village? It was the only all-wooden structure in the village for a very long time." The men all shook their heads, as Juan-Carlos knew they would. "Ah, well... the woman who ran it was very old even then, and as I've mentioned, I was only a very young boy. Of course, I was old enough to know numbers and amounts, and

I remember that she must have made very good money that week. All six rooms at her place were filled with all the scientists and other important people who came from the capital to study the phenomenon. In fact, I delivered some borrowed blankets to the boarding house, and I saw with my own eyes that she put the visitors three to a room, with two sleeping head to toe in the same bed and the third sleeping on a pallet on the floor."

He sighed, seeming disheartened for a moment. "Unfortunately, just as if it were our fault that we'd received an over-abundance of rain, we had no rain at all the whole next summer. In fact, the sun and the wind actually seemed to deduct moisture from us as restitution to whomever is in charge of rainfall. There was a disastrous result. Each day was hotter and drier than the last, and one scalding afternoon that boarding house burst into flame."

Jose asked, "Did it burn to the ground?"

Juan-Carlos shrugged and nodded. "Of course, or course. As you might imagine, both the structure and the old woman inside had been leached so thoroughly of moisture, the whole thing burned to the ground and blew away in the wind." He snapped his finger. "It was over just that quick. It was gone before the men could find so much as a bucket or any water to carry in it."

A few men laughed quietly and shook their heads, and Juan-Carlos seemed to take offense. He pointed his finger at them. "You laugh, and I understand—I really do—but I have proof, my friends. Tomorrow—but please come in the coolness of the morning—tomorrow if you will meet me here, I will walk with you to the former location of the lodging house. There, even if you get on your hands and knees with a glass that makes an ant look the size of a horse, you will see for yourself with your very own eyes that not so much as a trace of that boarding house remains." He nodded and put one hand on his chest. "I will do that for you because you are my friends and I want you to know you can trust me."

So goes an afternoon at the cantina in Agua Rocosa. I hope you will visit.

* * *
*

ABOUT THE AUTHOR

Gervasio Arrancado was born in a small shack in Mexico and raised in the orphanage at Agua Idelfonso, several kilometers, give or take a few, from the fictional fishing village of Agua Rocosa. He is fortunate to have made the acquaintance of Augustus McCrae, Hub and Garth McCann, El Mariachi, Forest Gump, The Bride (Black Mamba), Agents J and K, and several other notables. To this day he lives at that place on the horizon where reality just folds into imagination. Visit Gervasio on the web at Harvey Stanbrough & Friends Writing in Public, http://HEStanbrough.com.

Made in the USA
Las Vegas, NV
06 May 2022

48475525R00069